THE WEAVER AND THE WEB

CURSED: ARACHNE

OTHER BOOKS

Fated

The Head and the Heart

The Flower and the Flame

The Sorrow and the Sea

Cursed

The Princess and the Prophecy

The Fallow and the Faint

The Weaver and the Web

THE WEAVER AND THE WEB

CURSED: ARACHNE

KERRI KEBERLY

Cover design by Keith Robinson

Dragonfire Press

Print ISBN: 978-1-958354-83-4

CHAPTER 1

Little Arachne shivered when she slipped from the warmth of her bed and into the chill of night. There was no slumber to rub from her eyes, for she had not been sleeping. She had been lying awake for hours, thinking of how she would arrange the colored threads on her mother's loom.

She crept silently to the door that separated her family's home from the shop where they sold their wares. Her heart pounded in her chest, but it was not from fear of the dark like other children. She knew these rooms and short halls like the back of her hand. No, her pulse jumped in anticipation from what she was about to do.

They sold yarn dyed by her father and bolts of fine cloth weaved by her mother, the edges stitched and embroidered with silk thread by her older siblings. But of all the things sold in their shop, the intricate and colorful tapestries were Arachne's favorite.

From the time she could walk on her own, Arachne was eager to learn her mother's craft. She would stare transfixed as her older siblings would comb and spin wool or wind silk threads, annoying them with her endless questions. *When would she be a weaver like Mama?* was the one she asked most often.

Her heart would sink every time her sister would laugh at her, telling her she wasn't old enough to sit at the loom. *Why, her feet didn't even reach the floor when she sat on the stool!* Once her brother would join in the ribbing, Arachne would run crying to their *mama*, who would always stop what she was doing. She would take Arachne in her arms and pet her long dark hair, wiping away her tears as she gently reiterated what Arachne had already been told countless times; she was too small, too antsy, too this, and too that.

Perhaps it was being told no, or that Arachne was forbidden from doing something, but the denials only ignited a burning passion within her. She continued her relentless pursuit to become a weaver like her mother until she was finally given the task of grinding the dried plants and insects to make the dyes her father used. She would help him hang the colorful yarns and silk threads, and once they were dry, she would wind them onto the bobbins. She did this happily, watching her mother carefully as she did her work and learning what went where while she created wondrous scenes out of the threads Arachne and her father had prepared for her.

When Arachne had finally mastered spinning, dying, and winding, she was allowed to sit next to her mother and push the weft down with a wooden comb while her mother inserted the shuttle into the warp near the heddles. Arachne was quick, and it wasn't long before they fell into a rhythm, working as though they were one person with two pairs of hands.

Arachne knew she only slowed her mother down working this way, but with so many patrons coming into the shop, there was no time for her mother to oversee Arachne's work if she attempted a tapestry on her own.

She was not yet tall enough to reach the top of the loom. What if she made an error? What if the warp was too tight, or worse, too loose? They could not afford to waste the expensive wool! Those were the excuses her parents gave, even though she presented her case each morning.

"Mama, imagine having two weavers in the family!" she would say to her mother before rounding on her father, tugging on the back of his tunic as he worked. "Papa, think of how much more we could earn!"

Despite her insistence, they remained firm. "A few more years, daughter," her father would say, patting her on the head with a dye-stained hand. "Now run along. There is wool to be combed, and I must get back to my work."

Arachne would sigh, always careful to hide the sullen look on her face as she completed the day's chores, which included leaving the small town in which they lived each evening and going up into the grassy mountainside to help corral her grandfather's sheep for the night. It was a rite of passage; all her siblings had taken their turn at helping the old man.

On her way there, she would let her mind wander, smiling at the vibrant scenes she saw herself weaving inside her head. She supposed she couldn't blame her parents for their trepidation. They had the shop to run. In her opinion, that was even more reason to let her weave. After all, she was twelve now, and, besides that, she had waited long enough. She *knew* she could do it.

An adolescent bird simply knows when it's time to leave the nest, does it not?

Her innate sense of knowing wasn't the problem. It was convincing her mother and father to trust her. There was no other way to prove to them she could earn her keep than to take matters into her own hands. Like a bird ready to venture out into the open sky, she had waited until her parents were not around to test her wings for the first time.

A small flickering light filled the room when Arachne lit the oil lamp and then tip-toed over to the corner where her mother weaved each day. She sat the lamp on a wooden table before inhaling deeply. Tonight, Arachne would finish the tapestry her mother had begun. In the morning, her mother and father would praise her work, and she would finally be allowed to weave on her own.

Her gaze traveled over the half-finished tapestry, darting to the places where her mother had made small errors. No matter, they would be unnoticeable soon enough. Arachne bent to pick up the shuttle, grinning at the weight of it in her hand, and as she climbed onto the stool and began to weave, her lips widened into a grin.

CHAPTER 2

ARACHNE YAWNED, THE rosy fingers of dawn gently caressing her back. She'd worked through the night, her fingers moving so deftly, it had surprised even her. Both exhausted and exhilarated, she slipped off the stool to survey her work.

She couldn't wait for her mother to see how perfectly the threads had fallen into place. The patron who'd commissioned it was sure to be delighted. The tail feathers of the owl sitting atop Athena's shoulder were so intricate in their detail and wonderful in their dimension, they looked as though she could reach out and pluck one. The goddess's face and form so lifelike it seemed she'd come down from Olympus to grace the shop with her presence.

Arachne whirled around when she heard the gasp.

Her mother stood in the doorway, hand over her mouth and eyes brimming with tears before dropping her hand and hurrying over to inspect the tapestry.

"The gods..." she murmured, running her fingertips over the threads lightly. "It must be the work of the gods."

"No, Mama," Arachne shook her head, stepping closer. "It was me."

"Do not tell such tall tales, Arachne," replied her mother, sounding more fearful than unkind. "It is offensive to the gods."

"I'm not lying," insisted Arachne. "I worked all night so that you could see for yourself that what I say is true." She smiled triumphantly, wiggling her fingers playfully. "I am a weaver, just like you."

Her mother glanced at the oil lamp, smoke still curling up from the wick that had recently been extinguished. She fixed her eyes on Arachne once more. "You've been blessed by the gods with this talent."

Arachne beamed up at her, even though something heavy threatened to weigh the corners of her lips down. The gods had nothing to do with it. It had been her own two hands that had done the work. Her mind that had arranged the threads in both her dreams and in her waking hours. It was *she* who had learned how to weave, by carefully watching and patiently waiting, not the gods.

"What is all this commotion about?" came her father's voice. Before either of them could answer, he too gasped. "By the gods, Derya." He approached with wide eyes. "This is your finest work yet."

Arachne opened her mouth to set her father straight, but her mother spoke first.

"Idmon," she began, "Arachne has done this, not I."

His mouth dropped open, his gaze cutting to Arachne. "Is this true, child?"

Arachne nodded, heart thumping in her chest. Her head spun, and she thought it might explode from the few moments of stunned silence that followed, but she blew out a relieved breath from her lungs when her father began to laugh. It rang in the air with incredulity, his laughter, but the way he took her face in his hands and kissed each of her cheeks, it was clear he had chosen to celebrate the good fortune he'd woken up to and not scold his child for scandalous claims.

CHAPTER 3

BEFORE THE END of that year, Arachne had her own loom. Her father was a smart businessman, wasting no time capitalizing on the opportunity to have two weavers in his shop. This had not bothered Arachne or her mother. They both admired his gumption, for he was where Arachne got her resourceful and determined nature, and her mother had married a man who had always provided a good life for her, never raising a hand to her or their children. And so, Arachne and her mother worked side by side for the next six years, dutifully weaving the rugs and tapestries the townsfolk commissioned.

Arachne had never cared about the profits like her father, and still didn't. It was her work in which she cared most, and with each exclamation of joy and delight from another satisfied customer, she grew more certain she was doing what she was meant to do. The elation she felt whenever she began a new tapestry was only rivaled by the pride she felt when their mouths dropped open after seeing the end results.

Her attention to detail and eye for color was so keen, it wasn't long before the surrounding cities heard of the masterful young woman who wove even better than the best weavers far and wide, that wealthy patrons from all over Lydia came to commission larger and more elaborate scenes.

The years had passed, as they do, and her mother had begun to grumble about stiff fingers and aching joints. As she had slowed, it seemed Arachne had only gotten faster, completing her work in mere weeks instead of the months it normally took. It had been a blessing in disguise, really. A way for her mother to retire from her life-long craft with dignity, for no one was commissioning work from her any longer.

The crowds that normally gathered to watch Arachne weave were no exception on this morning. They murmured as they milled in and out of the shop, perusing the skeins of wool and bolts of fabric on display. Arachne paid them no mind. The din of busy city streets had become background noise to her. Instead, she focused her attention on the pretty trio of nymphs posing in front of her, just beyond her loom.

They had arrived several weeks ago, coming from the dense forests of the Hermus and

Caystor valleys and into the town of Hypaepa. The nymphs had personally sought her out because they wanted a gift to give to Artemis; a tapestry so fine the goddess of the hunt would cherish it above all other offerings.

"It must be done by the very best!" the golden-haired one had exclaimed.

"Then you have come to the right place," Arachne had replied, suppressing the urge to be mocking and disingenuous. In the beginning, such proclamations would cause Arachne's cheeks to redden. Over time, as her reputation as the most skilled weaver in all of Lydia grew stronger and the flattery, though still appreciated, began to have the opposite effect.

She had been wary of the nymphs at first. She did not have time for friendships, and she had wondered if the trio were truly nymphs as they said, or daughters of some wealthy politician playing pretend so they could save their father some coin. But their cheerful smiles and numerous compliments had eventually crumbled Arachne's walls, and over time she grew to trust them.

She believed in the divine, of course, but if the gods rarely showed themselves to mortals, why would nymphs and satyrs? Besides, it was too difficult for Arachne to believe that anyone would purposely deceive her, and so she chose to think they had forged a bond.

Whether they were mortal or nymph, her new friends had come every day to assume the same pose, remaining still for hours so Arachne could accurately capture each of their delicate features. Since the tapestry was to be a surprise for the goddess they worshipped, they could only describe her appearance to Arachne, who then wove the huntress standing stoically with her bow, surrounded by three adoring nymphs.

After pushing the last thread into place, Arachne set the shuttle in her lap and declared the tapestry finished. She waved a hand, beckoning the women over. "Come inspect my work, my friends, and let me know if you approve."

Arachne did not hide her smile. She knew they would find no flaws.

As if being released from invisible hands, the women rushed toward the loom, giggling and excited to see Arachne's handiwork. It was an airy sound, like birdsong carried on a breeze, and it forced Arachne to reassess the validity of their claim. Perhaps they were nymphs, after all. They had sat unmoving without food or water for many hours a day, for weeks. So still, in fact, it was as if time had stopped, freezing them into place.

"Oh, it's perfect!" exclaimed Celaeno, the dark-haired one, clasping her hands in front of her chest.

"It looks just like her," said the freckled-faced one, Morea, shaking her comely head in awed disbelief before nodding in whole-hearted approval. "She will be most pleased!"

Arachne tilted her chin upward, soaking in the praise. It revitalized her, for there was nothing more satisfying after so much time and effort than for accomplishments to be appreciated with such enthusiasm.

And then Pasithea, the one with the long golden waves, snatched away her good mood. "You have truly been blessed by the gods, my lady," she said, "and by the goddess of craft herself, no doubt!"

Arachne leveled a glare at the nymph who had rudely stolen her due. Irritation tightened her jaw, forcing her to speak through clenched teeth. "I beg your pardon, but Athena has had nothing to do with it. Your tapestry has been weaved by *my* hands, and mine alone."

The day's crowd suddenly went quiet. All except for a click of a tongue that came from behind Arachne. When she turned, there stooped a wrinkled old woman, leaning on her walking staff with cloudy eyes as gray as her wiry hair.

"Have your ambitions soared so high that you think you are equal to a goddess?" asked the old woman, her voice warbling and cracking with age. "That is a dangerous game to play, child."

Arachne's nostrils flared. Child? She was no such thing. Who on Earth did this old woman think she was to call the finest weaver in all of Lydia a *child?*

"I am a woman grown, and I play no games," said Arachne. "My work is unrivaled, even by divine hands."

"You dare speak such hubris?" The old woman shuffled forward, first one step, then two. "Your boast is a punishable crime, you know. If I were you, I would mind my tongue. The gods are not a forgiving lot when angered," warned the old woman. "Or so I am told."

Arachne could not stop herself from laughing. Clearly, this woman was not from Colophon nor Hypaepa, nor anywhere in Lydia for that matter. Ask anyone for hundreds of miles in every direction who the most sought out weaver was, and they would say Arachne.

Wherever this woman was from, she was delusional as well. To think she knew the gods personally was simply madness. Arachne tried to feel pity, but she could not. The annoyance that had burrowed under her skin had now turned into conceit that curled her lip.

"Let Athena come down and test my skill against hers if she is so bothered."

CHAPTER 4

ARACHNE HELD THE old woman's gaze defiantly. The woman did not speak, only stared back expressionless, which Arachne took for acquiescence. Satisfied the stranger had been put in her place, Arachne opened her mouth to speak, intent on dismissing the woman and dispersing the crowd so she could go back to her work. Instead, a shiver raced up her spine, spreading at the base of her skull before raking its cold fingers over her scalp.

Arachne narrowed her eyes. Were the deep lines and grooves surrounding the woman's piercing gray eyes disappearing? Was her lusterless gray hair ever so slowly turning vibrant with color?

Just then, a swirling mist arose. The air grew acrid with the smell of woodsmoke, stinging the inside of Arachne's nose. The heat of fire stifled the shop, and the dampness forming on her skin suddenly turned cold when the electric crackle of magic began to snap, answering her questions beyond a shadow of a doubt.

They were amid the divine, indeed.

As quickly as it had risen, the mist became a billowing fog, and Arachne blinked, trying not to cough as another question rose in her mind. Should she stand her ground or flee?

Whichever she could manage first, she decided, for the only thing that moved was the hair on her arms, and that was of its own accord. Despite feeling as though her feet were made of lead, she staggered backward, and through sheer force of will, waved away the cloying vapor with a hand. When the smoke finally cleared, her mouth dropped open at what—*who*—she saw standing before her.

Arachne gasped along with the others in the shop, who fell to their knees like raindrops when they saw how the old woman's spine had not only straightened but lengthened. They bowed their heads upon witnessing the gnarled wooden staff transform into a spear, and the faded, moth-eaten robes became a blinding white chiton under gleaming golden armor.

Athena peered down at Arachne with an arched brow. "How dare you set yourself above the gods."

Arachne swallowed hard. She had been brazened with her claims, and the goddess had caught wind of it. Offended, she had come down from Olympus disguised as an old woman to impart a warning instead of immediately striking Arachne down.

That meant she thought Arachne was formidable enough to address directly, did it not? There was only one way to find out.

Arachne reeled in her composure. First and foremost, Athena was the goddess of war. She was not known to be physically violent, although Arachne imagined she could be if provoked. No, Athena favored cunning and strategy over brute force, and so that was what Arachne would use to win this dangerous game in which she had found herself.

She would be the worthy opponent Athena thought her to be.

"I have said nothing about being better than the gods," Arachne replied coolly, even though her insides roiled. "Only that I am the best among mortals."

A ghost of a smile appeared on Athena's lips. "Then you admit you are not a better weaver than I, a goddess of Olympus?"

Arachne's defiant streak flared to life. How pretentious of Athena to assume Arachne would admit to something that simply wasn't true just because she was a mortal and Athena was a goddess.

"You misunderstand me, goddess. I can only admit to saying that here, among mortals, I am the best. Just ask any of these people who bow before you." Arachne gestured toward the crowd. She scanned the bobbing and turning heads until she found Celaeno.

Arachne locked eyes with her. "You there, didn't you say earlier how perfect this tapestry I weaved for you was?" Arachne walked over to the tapestry she'd finished less than an hour ago, only breaking eye contact to point at one of the woven nymphs dancing around Artemis. "That is you, is it not?" When Celaeno nodded helplessly, Arachne gestured toward the depiction of Artemis. "And here is the likeness of the goddess Artemis. One I believe you proclaimed to be perfect."

Arachne looked to Morea and Pasithea for confirmation, but they only whimpered, their eyes darting between Arachne and Athena.

"Hmm," sighed Arachne, turning to address Athena. "It seems your presence has made my friends too fearful to vouch for my skills." Arachne glanced at her mother's empty loom sitting in a darkened corner of the shop. "Perhaps we should have a contest, so you may see for yourself if what I say is true."

Athena glared at Arachne, who stared back. The gods were not always right. In fact, sometimes they were very, very wrong. Poseidon, Apollo, Hera, and Zeus. All led by their pride; even Athena herself had doled out unjust punishments at the slightest bruising of her ego.

This was Arachne's shop. These were her admirers. If Athena wanted proof that she was worthy of the adoration, she would give it. She had been born to be a weaver, dedicating her entire life to learning her craft, so that each scene she wove was perfect. Was it a gods-given talent? Perhaps, but the skills she had honed were through her own determination and focus, and she would be damned if she'd let a self-righteous goddess take the credit for that.

"Yes," agreed Athena. "Let us see who the better weaver is once and for all."

Arachne bowed her head, but only to hide how her nostrils flared with indignance. She would weave a tapestry, and it would be more beautiful and perfect than the conceited goddess of craft could ever imagine possible.

CHAPTER 5

Day One

ARACHNE GOT TO work removing Artemis's tapestry from her loom, quickly securing the ends and rolling it tightly before handing it over to Pasithea for safe keeping.

"Bring it back..." Arachne glanced at Athena, who had lifted her mother's old loom as though it were a feather and was now setting it down beside Arachne's. This is how she and her mother used to weave, side-by-side. Was the cunning goddess of strategy trying to get inside her head or her heart? Most likely both. "After the goddess has been humbled, and I will add a stronger border."

"Yes, my lady," whispered Pasithea, nodding sheepishly.

The other two women approached from behind Pasithea, Celaeno chewing on her lip as she wrung her hands.

"May Tyche bring you luck," whispered Morea, pulling Celaeno and Pasithea back toward the crowd.

They have no faith that I will win, thought Arachne. Her chest tightened, but she drew in a deep breath despite her laboring lungs. Likewise, the moment her eyes began to sting, she commanded her tears to remain at bay.

I will prove them wrong.

She had to. There was no other way around it. The goddess of craft had come down from Olympus and agreed to a contest that Arachne had initiated out of pride. She swallowed the lump forming in her throat. Mortals never fared well when challenging the gods. She had known that, so why had she done it?

Because it was high time someone showed the gods some humility.

Determined to spare no sign of worry, Arachne unclenched her teeth and smiled at the crowd reassuringly as she walked over to the baskets which held the array of colored threads she would use to best Athena.

Arms full of bobbins, Arachne took a seat. When she glanced over at Athena, already sitting at her mother's loom, she saw the goddess had chosen no threads. Was this another tactic meant to throw her off?

Very well, then. Two could play at that game.

"Forgive me, goddess," began Arachne, the thought forming in her mind as though Eris, the goddess of discord, whispered the words into her ear. "But if the contest is to successfully determine who the better weaver is, we must compete on equal footing." She gestured toward the baskets. "I am not divine, but I do have plenty of thread left to share."

Athena lifted her chin, rolling her eyes toward the sky and sighing. "So you do." With a wave of her hand, the baskets appeared at her side. "Any other rules you wish to impose?"

Arachne shook her head, ignoring the urge to point out that it wasn't a rule, but an observation, or how the goddess was trying to throw her off kilter with all her subtle manipulations.

"Shall we begin?" replied the goddess, arching her brow.

Arachne squeezed her hands together to stop them from shaking. She would not show weakness. That would only allow Athena to win before the contest even started.

"Wait," said Arachne, pleased her voice had not cracked, or worse yet, given out completely. "I do have a request."

"Of course you do," replied Athena, tilting her head and waiting for Arachne to disclose her petition.

Arachne took a steadying breath, glancing around the crowd before deploying a bit of her own strategy. "Unlike mortals, the gods do not need rest or sustenance. This contest will last for several days, at least, perhaps longer." The shop had gone silent, with all eyes on her as she spoke loudly enough for everyone to hear. "I ask you, good people of Hypaepa, what would it prove if I work myself to death? How will you declare a winner if my loom stands half empty while I lay starved?"

Murmurs rippled through the crowd, many heads nodding in agreement. Arachne suppressed a smile. She had struck two birds with one stone. Not only had she further evened the playing field, but she had also planted the seed of who would do the judging; the men and women she saw every day.

Arachne could feel Athena's irritation rolling off her. The goddess's ego was enormous, even bigger than Arachne's, and it pressed in on all sides, smothering all who stood in its way. Arachne suspected the townsfolk felt the weight of it as well. She only hoped they would be brave enough to tell the truth, even in the face of the goddess of war's wrath.

"Enough pandering to your audience," snapped Athena, shattering Arachne's thoughts. "What do you propose?"

Arachne cleared her throat. It was just as well, for she shouldn't get too far ahead of herself. "A small rug, depicting the scene of our choosing. We shall work for five days, no more, no less, leaving the loom to rest and refresh each evening. At the end of the fifth day, the fair people of Hypaepa will declare a winner."

A sound began low in Athena's throat, gathering strength before bursting forth in a resounding wave of laughter. "Your confidence, though admirable, is an illusion. You have no idea how greatly this amuses me, girl." A smile curled the goddess's lips, as cruel as a cat toying with its prey. "I agree to your terms."

"I am no girl." The words came out unbidden, as did the proud lift of her chin. She was tired of this battle of wits already. It was time to let her weaving speak for itself. "My name is Arachne."

The muscle over Athena's jaw ticked ever so slightly. "Well then, *Arachne*," she said through clenched teeth. "Let us begin."

CHAPTER 6

Day Two

SHADOWS CAST BY the oil lamps danced across the shop walls, indicating another day of weaving had come and gone. How could that be possible? Hadn't the sun rose mere hours ago?

Drained and sore, Arachne rubbed her eyes before leaning back to assess the day's progress. The ivy border was coming along beautifully. She frowned, even though the different shades of green made the vines look as though their pointed leaves were twisting off the loom.

She still did not know what scene she would weave.

Resisting the urge to look over at Athena's loom, Arachne stood, bending and stretching her aching fingers. "It is time to stop for the night."

The *tap, tap, tap* of Athena's weaving continued, and the goddess hummed lightly, ignoring Arachne and going about her work as though she had heard nothing.

Arachne had promised herself she would not so much as glance at the goddess, and she had done well so far, but her sense of fairness got the best of her, and she turned toward Athena, mouth open and ready to repeat her last words, more harshly if needed.

Arachne pressed her lips thin when she saw the border on Athena's loom. It was a golden meander, the linear pattern folding in on itself flawlessly. Her gaze drifted of its own volition to the bottom corner of the tapestry, where she saw the beginning of a scene that made her heart pound.

It was a goddess, to be sure, but which one Arachne could not tell. Whoever she was, it was clear by the way her hand rested atop the head of the mortal kneeling before her she was a divinity pardoning the mundane for some unknown—and most likely small—offense.

Arachne looked away, frustrated she had fallen into the trap. It had been calculated and set with mastery, for Athena had put down her shuttle without protest the previous evening, vanishing and going wherever it was goddesses go as soon as Arachne had suspended the contest until morning. This night, she had kept going, knowing full well it would goad Arachne into looking at her, and in the process, what was on her loom.

"It is time to stop for the night!" snapped Arachne, no longer caring if she offended the divinity beside her. The goddess wasn't exactly playing fair, so why should Arachne be polite?

"Oh, so it is," replied Athena, her words ripe with amusement and dripping with sarcasm.

Before Arachne could respond, the goddess disappeared. Her taunting laugh echoed from the ether, her mission to upset Arachne having been thoroughly accomplished. Arachne scoffed, angry at herself for breaking the one rule she'd been determined to keep: Do not, under any circumstances, give snide Athena a single ounce of satisfaction.

Judging by the smug grin on the goddess's face the moment before she disappeared, Arachne had not only given her an ounce of satisfaction, but also a pound of flesh.

Arachne headed for her room, avoiding the looks of pity from her mother and father as she picked up an oil lamp. Though they had been busy during the day, for the contest had drawn in gawkers and paying customers alike, they sat on their stools once the sun had gone down, offering moral support and silent encouragement until it was time for the competing weavers to stop for the night.

They showed no signs of disappointment as she passed by them, nor did they admonish her for being foolish enough to think she could best a goddess, and for that, Arachne was grateful. The pressure was becoming too much to bear. One word from them and Arachne might crack, and she could not afford to break apart now. They had barely just begun.

She unleashed a frustrated sigh once she was safely in her room, but nothing more. No lamenting and no tears. The goddess could be looking down upon her even now, relishing the show of weakness, feeding off Arachne's pain and growing stronger.

Arachne would simply not allow it.

She undressed, putting on her sleeping clothes even though she doubted she would close her eyes at all. She needed to think of a way to outdo Athena. After what Arachne had seen earlier, it was clear their technical skills were equally matched.

It felt good to lie down, until a yawn stretched her mouth wide, reminding her she was only human. She was no goddess, unhindered by mortal trappings such as hunger and thirst. Exhaustion. Even though she was young and healthy, at the very least, she needed food and rest to survive.

Almost immediately after blowing out the lamp, the image of Athena's unfinished scene found its way into Arachne's mind; the goddess pardoning the mortal. Oh, how highly the gods thought of themselves. How audacious to proclaim perfection in both word and deed when they, too, fell prey to emotions like jealousy and fear. What luck their power afforded them to act on impulse without judgment for their tantrums, whereas mortals were doomed to suffer the consequences.

Her lips pressed tight at the self-righteousness. Was it any wonder when they had a ruler like Zeus, the god who believed he was entitled to satisfy every lustful whim, whether it was welcomed or not? And Apollo, the god whom no one—divinity or mortal—escaped unscathed or uncursed when he did not get his way. He was petulant and pathetic; they all were...

The truth suddenly revealed itself to Arachne, causing her to gasp. That was it. Powers be damned, they *weren't* any better than mortals, and that was what they so desperately wanted to keep a secret, why they threatened anyone and everyone who challenged their supreme rule.

Arachne smiled in the dark, closing her eyes and feeling lighter than she had in days, the weight of her worry taking flight from her shoulders as quickly as a bird. She finally knew the perfect scene to weave, and tomorrow she would turn her loom toward the wall so that no one could see what she was doing until it was complete.

There was no rule that said she couldn't.

As she drifted off into a deep and dreamless sleep, Arachne thought of the look on the goddess's face when the time came to reveal their finished scenes. Arachne would win, not with her skill, for that was a draw, but with her cunning.

She would beat the goddess at her own game.

CHAPTER 7

Day Three

ON THE MORNING of the third day, neighbor stood next to neighbor, whispering to each other while the old sat gripping their walking sticks as they stared with rheumy eyes. The opportunistic held remnants of fabric, bought with the intention to travel to nearby towns and resell them. Regardless of the reason they were there, all waited anxiously for the challenge to resume, for the whole town had heard of the contest between mortal and goddess by then.

Arachne walked to her loom, accepting the nods of approval with a smile as the crowd parted for her. Her heart soared, as did her confidence, until she noticed Athena had not yet appeared. She pushed the thought away, and what it might mean, and turned the heavy structure toward the wall. Once the laborious task was complete, she went back for the stool, dragging it noisily as she wondered whether to begin her work or wait. Her luck, she would break some unspoken rule of the gods by starting before Athena, and the goddess would claim an unfair victory.

Arachne sat down and picked through her basket of thread to stall for time. She did not have to wait long. Athena breezed through the shop front and toward her loom, a chorus of excited giggles from the trio of nymphs harmonizing with her smug laughter ringing through the air.

"Of course I will weave something for you," Athena said loudly. "It shall be no trouble at all, once this inconvenient matter of my mastery has been settled, that is."

Arachne wanted to clap her palms over her ears. Instead, she ground her teeth, refusing to look in their direction. She couldn't bear witness to their fawning over the goddess, all rosy-cheeked and flushed from her attention. Hadn't they proclaimed *Arachne* was the best? How fickle they were, tripping over themselves to flatter Athena when it was Arachne they curried favor with only days ago. How feckless and disloyal of them to switch sides so easily.

Arachne bit down on her lip until she tasted blood, inflicting physical pain to stop the torment in her heart. They had never been her friends all along.

Without another moment of delay, Arachne cleared her mind, blocking everyone and everything out to focus solely on her weaving. She proceeded to let the hurt fuel her fire, for she would reveal the truth. The divinities of Olympus were nothing more than petulant children, incapable of any real self-reflection or true magnanimity. The gods and goddesses demanded sacrifices and worship yet continued to go back on their promises, smiting the hands that fed them without care or concern. Whether Arachne won or not, when she finished, everyone would see their hypocrisy in living color.

Her fingers moved with renewed fervor, her mind alive and crackling and resolute. She would work the night through, if need be, but Athena would be humbled if it was the last thing Arachne ever did.

She could feel Athena glare at her from time to time, vexed, no doubt, that Arachne saw the wisdom of moving past the provocations, paying no mind to the piercing jabs the goddess sent her way. Likewise, she ignored the wounds they left, for no doubt some people were only there, watching her every move, to see if she would make a mistake.

Although she tried not to let it, with each sidelong glance, each whispered word, Arachne's self-assurance trickled from each cut left by the goddess.

Athena's actions were deliberate, which was why, even though Arachne's belly twisted in knots, she was determined to continue as though she were unbothered. Let the goddess try and get inside her head, so that she might fail. It would only prove her point. The gods and goddesses of Olympus were jealous and petty, resorting to intimidation to achieve the outcome they desired, and not the paragons of altruism they claimed to be.

The nymphs were proving to be no better. Arachne's mouth watered when they spread out a blanket in front of her and proceeded to eat handfuls of nuts and berries, allowing the juice of ripe nectarines to run down their arms as they gorged themselves.

Arachne pulled her empty stomach tight, to muffle its growling when the sweet scent of the fruit reached her nostrils. Even Celaeno, no longer shy, had found it within herself to engage in such mean-spirited behavior. Tears welled in Arachne's eyes at how heartbreaking it was that such gentle souls could be swayed to be so needlessly cruel.

Arachne's mother must have had the same thoughts. Without a word, she got up from her stool and disappeared into their home. A few minutes later, she returned with a small loaf of bread and a jug of water.

"Open," said her mother. "I will feed you bit by bit, so that you do not have to stop."

Arachne shook her head, mortified, but her mother insisted.

"Do not be stubborn, daughter. Let me help you." Her mother tore a small piece from the loaf and gestured for Arachne to open her mouth. "You must be strong."

Her mother spoke truth, there was no denying it. She was mentally and physically exhausted, and if she was to be honest with herself, close to conceding. It was either accept this support and keep going or refuse and risk defeat. Arachne obeyed her mother and opened her mouth, grateful for the intervention.

"You are good and kind and valued, Arachne," whispered her mother, handing over the water jug. "Do not let them make you think otherwise." She took Arachne by the chin, lifting her gaze to meet her own. "The only person to whom you must prove your worth is you. Do your best, for it will always be enough for those who love you, and that is all that matters."

CHAPTER 8

Day Four

ARACHNE AWOKE THE next morning at dawn, renewed by her mother's wise words. It was early enough for the sky to be dim and the shop empty, but it would be full soon, and she longed for a few moments of quiet solitude before the crowd began to gather. She sat the lamp down and pulled off the cloth she'd been draping over her loom each night. After folding it, she set it aside and retrieved the lamp, holding its glowing light up to the nearly finished tapestry to survey her work.

It was her finest yet, in both skill and theme.

"Now, why do you suppose she would cover her loom when she knows I could simply remove it with a flick of my wrist?" came Athena's voice.

Arachne flinched, startled by the intrusion. Her gaze cut to Athena, who stood stoically by her own loom, surrounded by her unearthly cohorts.

"Perhaps she has gone mad," quipped Pasithea, all sweetness gone from her voice as she pulled out a stool for Athena.

Their features seemed more sharp, sinister even, and with each thud of her racing heart, the hair on Arachne's arms rose higher. She had hoped for a fair competition, but that was not to be. She shivered, gooseflesh pinching her skin taut before releasing and smoothing again.

She had no defense against the accusation—she *had* felt like a madwoman these past few days—and so she did not plead her case. Instead, she sat at her loom without saying a word.

"Or maybe," said one of the nymphs, which one Arachne did not know, for she refused to look at any of them. "She's gone mute."

The nymphs, who she had thought were her friends, guffawed loudly, causing a hurt so immense to rise within Arachne she nearly crumpled. She pressed the balls of her feet into the ground, steadying the dizziness that plagued her. Although she ceased her swaying, her cheeks continued to blaze with embarrassment, betraying her just as thoroughly as the nymphs had.

It didn't take long for the three of them to erupt into another round of giggles. Their laughter scorched away Arachne's embarrassment, leaving anger in its place to beat against her temples with excruciating force.

Why must they keep adding insult to injury? Enough, already!

She had done nothing to deserve this never-ending torment. Her only crime had been being born with a talent for weaving. Was she to downplay her skill? Hide her keen eye? Turn away those who sought her out? Abandon the one thing that gave her purpose, all to spare the delicate feelings of another?

Athena had ordained herself the best weaver on both Olympus and in the mortal world. Clearly, she could not bear the thought of being usurped by a powerless mortal woman. Was she so insecure she would resort to maleficence to hold onto her reign as Goddess of Craft?

Or was her ego simply that fragile?

Arachne fumed at the thought, griding her teeth so furiously she thought she might crack the lot of them in half. Only her common sense stopped her from jumping up from her stool in a blind rage and grabbing the nymphs by their long hair and throwing them out of her shop. She would no doubt scream obscenities as she cast them far from her vicinity, forbidding them from re-entering.

As satisfying as it would feel, it would be a dangerous endeavor. There were three of them, four counting the goddess, against one. Though her parents would undoubtedly assist her in tossing the wretched creatures out by their ears, they were human, unable to withstand the goddess's magic that would surely strike them dead should Arachne dare such a bold move.

To that end, she remained seated, tamping her fury down just far enough so that she could loosen her jaw. She drew in several calming breaths, exhaling slowly and expelling the loathing that filled her to the brim.

She did not manage to release all of it, but at least enough to realize there would be no use in responding. They would continue their teasing, and she would let them. They could believe what they wanted, she would ignore them and go about her weaving as though they were not there. Their goading would soon be lost in the noise of spectators talking over one another, and she would be glad for it. If she could not hear it, she would not be tempted to seek justice for the pain and suffering it caused.

Arachne began to weave, focusing on the scene before her. She pulled the heddles, then laced the threads through the weft, over and under until everything around her faded away. To her, weaving was like breathing, and she lost herself in the movements. Before long, she was so engrossed in her work, she hardly noticed when the spectators had begun to arrive.

She remained in her meditative trance for the entire day, barely noticing anything around her. She knew some things, however; the sun had crested high in the sky before sinking beneath the horizon in what felt like mere minutes. And when night fell, she was aware of how she kept working by the light of the lamp her mother had lit for her. In fact, it was Athena who was now calling for the contest to suspend for the evening.

Arachne set down her shuttle, teetering on her stool as she rubbed her weary eyes with bone-tired fingers. She scanned the tapestry, which was nearly completed, a smile curling her lips as she sat admiring her work. Let them say whatever they wanted about her. She knew in her heart of hearts she was a talented weaver.

She stood abruptly, wasting no time fetching the cloth from the corner and throwing it over the loom. Athena had already disappeared, and the few who had remained were gone, but she would take no chances. She watched as the thin fabric settled over the frame, hiding her progress from prying eyes while she slept. She would reveal her work only when ready, and not a moment before.

With a satisfied sigh, Arachne picked up the oil lamp and headed toward the door. The next evening, the contest would be over, and so, too, would life as she knew it. After tomorrow, she would be known as the mortal woman who had challenged a goddess and won.

CHAPTER 9

Day Five

THE FIFTH DAY started like the previous four; Arachne awaking at first light with a churning in her belly. Once her upset stomach was settled with watered wine, figs, and bread, she entered the shop and pulled the cloth from her loom. No sooner did she sit when Athena appeared, dressed in a pristine battle tunic under gleaming armor. Atop her head rested a helmet.

Athena made a show of removing her head piece, shaking out her lustrous hair to elicit murmurs of adoration from the quickly gathering crowd. Arachne nearly rolled her eyes at the absurdity of the display. She didn't know whether she wanted to laugh hysterically or unleash a maniacal scream. She settled on a low grumble under her breath when Athena took a seat.

Arachne worked diligently throughout the afternoon, soothed by the steady clicking and tapping that punctuated the din of the crowd. This was the last day, and more people than ever had come from far and wide to see how the contest would end.

To her surprise, and considering her theatrics that morning, Athena remained quiet. Unusually so. There was no goading from her or the nymphs, and the absence of it made Arachne shift uneasily. She had grown accustomed to fending off the goddess's constant psychological warfare.

Finally, curiosity got the better of her, and Arachne glanced over at the goddess. If nothing else, she told herself, it was to make sure she was still there. She was, and Arachne's stomach plummeted when she saw Athena's lips curled into a smug smile, clearly pleased.

Arachne quickly looked away, disappointed in herself for expecting to see something different. Of course, Athena's lips would not be pressed together in vexation. Her work was beautifully crafted, in plain sight for all to see.

She only does it to trick your mind into believing the worst, thought Arachne as she set her jaw. Determined not to let the goddess's tactics derail her so close to the end, Arachne ignored whatever machinations Athena employed now and kept going, taking her time and not letting herself get rushed into making a mistake.

A little while later, a satisfied chuckle came from Athena's side of the shop. Arachne knew it could only mean one thing. Athena had finished, and well before the purple haze of twilight had begun to appear. After a few minutes, the goddess sighed, impatient at having to wait for Arachne, and rose from her stool to pace with folded arms.

Arachne peered at her surreptitiously, following her as she walked back and forth. When the nymphs flocked to her side to compliment the fine fit of her armor, Athena relished their flattery, but her smile was thin and her uplifted mood fleeting.

Arachne's own lips tipped upward. Could Athena be nervous?

Arachne shook away the thought, unable to afford such hope. She kept her expression placid, taking care not to get caught eavesdropping, or worse, sympathizing.

No, she must not become distracted now, not when she was so close to winning. But the way Athena's brow creased, trying to hide how she nipped at the inside of her cheek with her teeth, made her look almost human, and Arachne could not help but feel a little sorry for the goddess.

Not so sorry she would offer comfort, however. Athena had put her through too much for her to be moved enough to show pity. Besides, there was no sense in trying to make friends with the goddess now. Like the nymphs, the goddess had already shown her true colors.

The golden afternoon light soon faded to a burnt orange dusk. Thankfully, Arachne's steadfastness had served her well, as she was nearly done. With only a few more rows to tap into place, she could call her work finished.

When Arachne set down her shuttle, the crowd went silent.

"Are you finally finished then, Arachne?" asked Athena.

Arachne cleared her throat. "Yes."

"Well, then, let us make haste in presenting our work to the judges." Athena looked pointedly at the crowd. "So they can say which of us will be victorious."

Arachne stood, smoothing her wrinkled skirts before stepping forward. She clutched the side of her loom for support as she gestured toward Athena's tapestry. "Please do us the honor of going first."

Arachne's gaze cut to Athena's tapestry a moment later, having no choice but to truly look upon it since the contest had begun. She swallowed hard at what she saw.

Four scenes, one in each corner: Antigone as a stork, her curse cast by the hand of Hera; Rhodope and Haemus turned into mountains by Zeus; Gerana, the queen of the Pygmies who dared to claim her beauty surpassed even that of Hera, in the middle of changing into a crane; Zeus transforming Myrrha into a petrified tree, obliging her request to become anything other than human to atone for her sins.

Each portrayed mortals being punished by the king and queen of the gods for their hubris, reminding all who gazed upon the scenes of the gods' power and majesty. The tapestry was magnificent, utterly flawless in its execution, and indeed rivaled Arachne's own craftsmanship.

But it wasn't the perfection of the renderings that made Arachne's blood boil in her veins.

In the center, much more imposing than the rest, was the contest between Athena and Poseidon. The scene showed the goddess's victory over her uncle; how cunning she was that she could prevail over one of the most fearsome gods on Olympus.

"All things come from the gods," warned Athena, lifting her chin. "And all things can be taken away by them."

Unlike Arachne, who had turned her loom so that no one could see the progression of her work, Athena had been weaving her tapestry for all to see. Yet, the wide-eyed and open-mouthed expressions of shock and awe on the people's faces made it seem as though they had just now seen it for the very first time.

Athena glared at Arachne, who stared back into her glittering gray eyes. The goddess no doubt assumed Arachne's submission would not compare, and that victory was already hers.

But the goddess was mistaken.

Wooden legs scraped across hard-packed earth as Arachne turned her loom around to reveal her tapestry.

"That may be true," began Arachne, stepping aside so that all could see, "but are they taken away justly?"

Gasps of shock rippled through the crowd. Arachne ventured to guess it was the way the images of the gods—Apollo, Dionysus, Cronos, Zeus— engaged in their amorous adventures seemed to leap off the loom as though happening before their very eyes.

Adventures was not the right word; lustful trysts were more fitting, and only a few of many could be depicted at that, for all their hypocrisies could not possibly fit on one tapestry.

Whether it was from exhaustion, triumph, or fear, Arachne felt as though she might faint. She inhaled a steadying breath, forcing herself to remain standing. She did not want to miss the way Athena's eyes scanned her masterfully weaved scenes, nor how far her jaw dropped when she fully grasped their meaning.

Arachne may not have surpassed Athena in weaving skills, but she had certainly outdone her with the very thing in which the goddess also took great pride: strategy. Arachne had bested Athena not with the prowess of her hands, but with the cleverness of her mind.

"What say you, good people of Hypaepa?" said Arachne. "Have the gods prevailed today?" She paused for effect, tilting her head and looking directly into Athena's eyes, even though she knew she should not. "Or have they discovered they are as powerless as mortals against the brutal grip of jealousy, lust..." Arachne raised a brow, for there was no going back now. And why should she? She had won. "And pride."

Athena's pupils shrank into pinpoints of rage, her mouth snapping shut before screwing into a vicious sneer. The crowd shrieked in unison, clambering this way and that until stranger clung to stranger in the wake of Athena's impeding fury.

CHAPTER 10

THE WALLS OF the shop trembled, as did the earth beneath Arachne's feet. Clumps of dirt rained down from the roof, shaken apart and falling to the ground, much like her short-lived victory.

"How dare you set yourself above the gods," seethed Athena, gray eyes flashing with indignance, outrage barely contained behind clenched teeth. "You have not heeded my warning and now you must pay the price."

Anger and disbelief tightened Arachne's chest, squeezing her lungs so tightly she could scarcely breathe. She had ended up like the mortals on Athena's tapestry, and in this moment, it was abundantly clear the contest had been for naught. The goddess would remain triumphant by any means, claiming victory one way or another. It did not matter that Arachne had succeeded in winning this battle; Athena would always win the war.

The injustice of it lent Arachne the strength she needed to lock her knees and stiffen her spine. "What crime have I committed? Please do tell, just and honorable goddess," she replied, no longer afraid of what retribution lay ahead of her.

Hadn't she known deep down it would come to this, that Athena would not accept defeat with even a shred of humility? That challenging her could have led to only one outcome. Arachne's downfall had been inevitable, and she had been too blinded by her need for fairness to see it.

"Insolence," said Athena, lifting her chin. "It is I who grants the gift of craft. If not for me, no one would even know your name. Yet, instead of being grateful for your talent, you offend me with your hubris."

Arachne barked with laughter, regretting she had been unable to control her outburst for only a heartbeat before giving in to her resentment. She would venture to speak her mind. True, she could—*should*—cease this useless endeavor of making the goddess see to reason. Yes, she should abandon this dangerous folly and back down, bowing low and thanking the goddess for allowing her such grace. But she would not. Could not, for she had already thrown the last of her caution into the wind when she dared to question the goddess outright.

More than that, now her reputation was at stake.

She could tolerate having her victory stripped away, but she could not bear being branded a braggart and a liar. She must at least save face with the people of Hypaepa, and she would do that by making sure they all understood the hypocrisy of the gods.

"Insolence or speaking plainly?" Arachne stepped forward, using the truth as her shield. "What helpless creature will you turn me into for a my terrible afront of being as good a weaver as you, goddess? A talent you yourself assert to have bestowed upon me!" She opened her arms wide, addressing the terrified and cowering crowd to further make her point. "What do you think, my fellow inferior and ever-obedient mortals? A bird? A dog?"

"Arachne," cried her mother, trying to push through the crowd.

Arachne had no doubt it was to clamp a hand over her mouth, to save her by preventing her from saying anything else. But it was too late for that. The goddess had taken too much from Arachne for her to care whether she lived or died now.

Reckless and wild with fury, she whipped her head toward Athena again and hissed, "A hideous gorgon?"

The goddess bared her teeth, unleashing an earsplitting shriek as she lunged, a shuttle appearing in her upraised hand. Each blow that came down upon Arachne was harder than the last, and when her legs finally buckled, she fell to the ground, curling into a ball and protecting her head with her hands. After a few more stinging blows to her back and shoulders, Athena stopped beating Arachne with her shuttle, but she knew the goddess was far from done.

Arachne heard the crack of bone before she felt the pain. Once she realized what was happening, she cried out in agony as the goddess crushed her fingers.

It took shattering every bone in her hands for Athena's rage to be sated. When the physical damage had been done, she knelt beside Arachne, grabbing a fistful of her hair and pulling her head back so that she could look at Arachne's swollen face as she delivered insult to injury.

"You thought yourself clever, didn't you?" said Athena. "Listen close and hear me well, *no one* is more cunning than I. Not my father, nor my uncle, and certainly not you, mortal. You're lucky my victory has left me feeling merciful. Be grateful the only things you lost this night were your hands and your pride."

Arachne's head thudded onto the hard ground when Athena let go of her hair. Bruised and bloodied, she tucked her mangled hands to her chest and wept. She had gone from bold winner to humiliated loser, utterly broken in more ways than one.

Her temples and her hands throbbed in tandem, and she whimpered from the excruciating pain as the edges of her vision slowly dimmed. Her head spun without mercy, and she longed for the blessed stillness of unconsciousness to overtake her. Then, as her world faded to black, there came an awful ripping sound, echoing in her ears as it followed her into the darkness.

CHAPTER 11

THE CEILING CAME into focus slowly. The room was dark, but Arachne could still make out the rough-hewn wooden beams of her home. For a moment, she thought she was staring up at them from her bed, but that wasn't right. She felt as though she were floating, weightless as a feather, while dozens of tiny lights swirled in and out of her vision.

She squinted at the glowing specks, following their fluid movements. No sooner had she thought she must be dreaming when a face materialized before her eyes. She shrank back in horror, for it was Athena scowling at her, a bloodied shuttle clutched in her raised fist, ready to strike again.

Now you must pay the price...

Even though the goddess's lips did not move, the words rang loudly in Arachne's ears. The shuttle came crashing down and Arachne screamed, jerking violently from the searing pain that racked her body.

"Shh-shh-shh," came a voice, deep and familiar and soothing. "She is gone. You are safe."

Arachne blinked. It was her father she saw now, his bearded cheeks wet with tears. She had never seen him weep and did not like that he was doing so now. Though, she could not deny she was relieved he still cared enough, despite the ruin she had surely brought down upon their family.

Arachne squeezed her eyes shut, but it was no use. Memories of the beating she had endured from Athena flooded her mind. She whimpered, her head lolling to the side. She sank further into her father's arms as he carried her. Where he would take her—home, the healer, or the nearest cliff from which to fling her broken body—she did not care, as long as it was far away from her pain.

When Arachne awoke for the second time, it was her mother she saw. She did not know how long she had been lost inside her dreamless sleep, but it had been long enough for the gray in her mother's hair to whiten her temples.

"Arachne?" said her mother, the cloth she had been using to wet Arachne's lips still poised over the bowl of water. "Arachne!" It dropped with a splash, and a moment later she was at Arachne's side, tears of joy welling in her eyes. "Idmon! Come! She's awake!"

Arachne winced at her mother's shouting. Her head throbbed, but she was glad for the dull ache of mending bones rather than the stabbing pain of broken ones.

Her father rushed into the room wiping purple dye from his hands and onto his leather work apron. Arachne's mouth tipped up at the corners. If he was still dyeing cloth, it could only mean one thing; the shop had not been lost.

Her smile dropped when her mother helped her sit up. Her own hands, still splinted and bandaged, were useless. Even though the bruises had faded, it would be a long time before she would be able to do anything for herself.

"Daughter," said her father, sitting on the edge of the bed near her feet. "It is good to see you finally awake."

"How long was I...?" A lump formed in her throat, forcing her to abandon her question.

Did she even want to know?

Her father glanced at her mother, who sighed before nodding. "A fortnight."

Arachne swallowed again, guilt dropping into the pit of her stomach like a stone. So long?

What had transpired in her absence? What sort of gossip had the town whispered? Was it in favor of her family or the goddess?

Bile rose in Arachne's throat. Judging by her parents' faces, she already knew the answer. She should never have been so brazen, for if it hadn't cost them already, it soon would.

"Has anyone—"

"I've started weaving again," said her mother cheerfully, cutting her off before she could finish her question, which was just as well since she herself didn't know what she would have asked. She did know, however, that her mother's smile did not reach her eyes. It was much too thin to hide whatever was being left unsaid.

"What is it?" asked Arachne.

"Rest," replied her mother. Instead of answering Arachne's question, she picked up the bowl once more. "I will bring you something to eat."

Arachne did not want to rest, nor eat. She wanted answers. She wanted to know why her mother's hands shook and her father was acting so strange.

If they would not tell her, she would go see for herself. She kicked the blankets from her legs, holding her hands out in front of her awkwardly.

"There is no need to worry." Her father stood abruptly, stepping backward to avoid an accidental strike to the chest as Arachne freed herself. "We will manage, daughter."

Her father's words only made her struggle harder to get up.

"Please, Arachne, calm down," pleaded her mother, setting the bowl on the table once again so she could take Arachne by the shoulders and gently push her back down onto the bed. "You must continue to heal."

"You are hiding something," said Arachne, panting from the exertion. "I know it. What is it?"

Her mother averted her gaze, suddenly more interested in straightening the crumpled covers tangled around Arachne's legs.

"What is it?" repeated Arachne. When her mother still refused to meet her gaze, she fixed her eyes on her father. "Tell me."

Her father sighed, closing his eyes briefly as he pinched the bridge of his nose. When he opened them, they held a sadness in them so profound it frightened her.

"Help her up, Derya." His voice was thick with weariness. "She will know eventually."

CHAPTER 12

ARACHNE STOOD WITH her mouth agape, stunned at what she saw. The shop was not full of patrons grumbling as they haggled for the best price like she had hoped. It was empty. The only people grousing within its walls were her siblings, eyeing her sulkily from where they sat combing or spinning wool.

She couldn't blame them. Their lowered status in the community was her fault. She had challenged a goddess knowing full well how much it could cost her. Should her family become destitute because of her egregious error in judgment, their poverty would fall upon her shoulders.

Arachne's bottom lip quivered as she scanned the countless stacks of cloth her father had artfully arranged on tables in order to catch the eye of passersby. Likewise, covering the floor were colorful rugs her mother must have woven while Arachne lay in bed healing.

She bit back a sob. She had no doubt her whole family had worked themselves to the bone for the last few weeks. The weariness in her father's voice. The trembling in her mother's hands. The stares from her siblings. And for what? Nothing, it seemed. They were all just as frightened about their future as she now was.

Why hadn't the people of Hypeapa banned together, buying extra cloth and rugs to help their own? Did it mean they were afraid of Athena or that they agreed with her? Did they think the cloth dyer's daughter was an arrogant fool, and doing business with him would anger Athena? Whatever their thoughts, they would be complicit in her impending ruin. It was clear they would abandon her and her family in a time of hardship instead of supporting them.

Arachne's gaze went from pile to pile and then to every corner of the shop until she found what she was looking for. It was not guilt that bubbled in her stomach when she found it, but anger.

"Why is it still here?" said Arachne, nodding at the loom standing near the entrance to the shop. She could understand why they'd kept one; her mother had needed it to weave the rugs. But the other? And displayed in a place of such prominence, for all to see as they walked past?

Arachne wanted it gone.

"The goddess forbade us to remove it," whispered her mother, wringing her hands as though it would stop her tears from forming.

"Get rid of it," said Arachne through clenched teeth, hardly able to look at Athena's tapestry without screaming.

"There is nothing to be done," said her father. "You were on the brink of death. We begged Athena to spare your life." He nodded toward Athena's tapestry. "And this was the price we agreed to pay. It must be kept on display."

Arachne's head spun, and her vision swam. She held onto her mother, who was so terrified, she shook. Or was Arachne shaking from anger? Judging by her father's heaving chest and the way his knuckles whitened from gripping the doorway, he was also struggling with his emotions.

At the cruelty of Athena's bargain or his daughter's wrath at taking it, she could not tell.

Arachne's heart softened, but the set of her jaw did not. It hardened. Right now, she did not care about the past. She was angry at the injustice of their future.

So very, very angry.

"Where is mine, then?" said Arachne, her voice pitched high and tight. She sounded like an entranced oracle, or a crazed madwoman. She felt like both; rambling and insane, and unable to stop herself from spewing nonsense. "If she is to have hers here, to serve as a reminder of her ill-gotten victory, it is only right that mine stand beside hers as a reminder of her hypocrisy." Arachne lifted her chin. "And her jealousy."

Her mother's gaze darted between her father and the corner, frantic and unknowing what to do next, but when he looked away, her hunched shoulders dropped in resignation.

"It is over there," she said, pointing toward the second loom.

Arachne's brow furrowed in confusion. "Where?" she said, peering into the darkness of the corner for her work of art. They would have had to remove it so her mother could weave her rugs, but surely, they would have folded it and stored it somewhere safer than a dark and dusty corner.

As she drew closer, the outline of something familiar appeared. Arachne's lungs labored in her chest, her mind trying to make sense of what she was seeing; deep within the recesses of the corner was tucked a basket.

Heart pounding, she lifted it with bandaged fingers and peered inside. At first, she couldn't comprehend what she saw; scraps of fabric, tangled up in long lines of fraying threads.

And then, when she realized the goddess had destroyed more than her hands, that she had also taken her livelihood and her dignity, she shook with rage.

Athena had ripped Arachne's tapestry to shreds.

CHAPTER 13

ARACHNE HAD NO way of knowing how many tears she had cried after seeing the physical embodiment of what Athena had done to her. They had fallen endlessly, it seemed, for like her greatest accomplishment, the goddess and her minions had torn her apart. For a long time, she was nothing more than a tangled mess, breaking down until the person she had been before no longer existed.

Alas, the months passed, and with each time she thought she was too broken to go on, Arachne willed the pieces of her life back together. Eventually, her hands healed, though they were never quite the same. They were gnarled and crooked, like that of an old woman, but, as painful as the process was, she slowly regained use of them until she could spin wool and wind bobbins. After some time, she could even prepare the loom for her mother by threading the weft. It was the small movements, the ones requiring dexterity, with which she still had trouble. But she was determined to weave once more, and so she continued to push herself.

Mourning doves cooed their sad song as Arachne stood on the street outside the shop early one morning, stretching and clenching her stiff fingers. The rigorous movements always made her wince, but what caused even more pain was the way the townsfolk avoided eye contact as they walked by. Some of them felt sorry for her, offering a quick nod before hurrying past, but most turned up their nose, dismissing her as though she were an errant dog.

She stayed faithful to her morning ritual despite this, just as she remained hopeful that one day soon, she would sit at the loom and surprise them all. She had done it before, and she would do it again.

Arachne smiled at a little girl walking next to her mother on the other side of the street. The girl smiled back, too young to know the celebrity Arachne had been and the pariah she was now. It was a sad thing, how far she had fallen from grace, but Arachne had found she could wallow in her misery for only so long before she must accept her fate and get on with her life.

Her heart thumped in her chest when the girl tugged on her mother's skirts, pointing at the shop. Arachne's stomach dropped when the woman stopped, bending to listen and then shook her head before taking her daughter by the arm and rushing off.

Arachne sighed. It had been almost a year of being ostracized, and their circumstance had become more dire with each waxing and waning of the moon. Another had capitalized on her family's decline by setting up a textile shop down the street. His wares were not as finely crafted, but it did not matter. The people of Hypeapa were as superstitious as they were devout. Not only would it displease the gods to do business with Arachne and her family; it would anger them.

She pursed her lips as she made her way inside the shop. Thanks to her ill-conceived delusions of grandeur, they had all witnessed the result of divine fury. And her father's business had suffered because of it.

Once inside, Arachne shook out several rugs before piling them onto a small cart. This had become her routine, peddling their wares in the market at the center of town. As impossible as it seemed, her sister had found a husband. He had been willing to marry her on the condition his family would receive an abundance of fine cloth and rugs as part of her dowry. Her parents had no choice but to agree, and on her sister's wedding day, the groom's relatives descended upon the shop like locusts. They took nearly everything.

It was some time before Arachne and her parents could replenish the shop, for her younger brother had fallen in love with a sweet-natured local girl and spent most of his time convincing her to marry him. With persistent declaration of his desire to marry for love and not wealth, she quickly agreed. Naturally, her family threatened to disown her if she became the wife of a disgraced dyer's son. Arachne's brother did not demand a dowry, which helped his cause tremendously, and finally, they were wed. After a small ceremony, they left the city, settling in the country and taking over their ailing grandfather's herd of sheep.

Her siblings had left Arachne, but she did not begrudge them for it. Had she not been responsible for the family's decline, she would have done the same. In fact, when Arachne was not preparing wool for weaving, or selling in the marketplace, she helped her brother tend to the large herd. It was mostly out of guilt, but seeing as her sister-in-law was now pregnant, it was also out of necessity. There was no way the girl could take care of their bedridden grandfather alone.

Lost in her thoughts, Arachne didn't notice the man approaching her.

"Arachne," he drawled, stepping in front of her and forcing her to stop. "How does this morning find you?"

The cart crashed into her back, and she released a small grunt of pain as she glared at the man for imposing. If a weasel could talk, it would sound just like Leon, the shopkeeper making his fortune off her family's undoing. She pushed the cart backward, maneuvering it so she could go around.

"Wait!" exclaimed Leon, holding up his hands. "I have a proposition for you..." He glanced down at the rugs in her cart, a grin spreading across his face. Arachne hated herself for noticing the fullness of his lips. He might be handsome, enough that she might have even entertained a courtship, but she could not look past the fact that he benefited off her family's demise.

She stifled the urge to drop the cart so she could slap one of his smooth cheeks.

"I want no dealings with you, Leon," she replied, pulling the cart forward.

"Ah, I see," he said, jumping out of the way to follow alongside her. "So, you are doing well and in no need of help, then?" He spun around to walk backward for a few paces before facing forward again and gesturing at her cart. "Or are these the same rugs you've been trying to sell for months?"

Arachne ground her teeth. Of course they were the same rugs. He *knew* they were.

She stopped abruptly, dropping the handles to fold her arms over her ribs. "What are you suggesting?"

"A mutually beneficial proposition," he said, arching an eyebrow. "A business venture of sorts…"

Arachne swallowed hard, praying it wasn't a marriage proposal. She couldn't marry him. Comely or not, Leon had proven to be opportunistic and greedy. The writing was on the wall, and she saw it clearly; the only property her family had left was the shop, which he would surely demand as a dowry. They would be doomed if he acquired more property, for it was power in a small town like Hypeapa. Moreover, there was no guarantee he would be a good husband or kind son-in-law. Arachne and her parents could very well end up in a worse situation than they were now.

They could be used and abused, driven to work without rest or little to say in the matter. Once he got his hands on her family's shop, he would undoubtedly find a way to gain control of the farm her grandfather had passed on to her brother. She cherished her brother, but he was a lover and not a fighter.

Arachne shivered. No, she would not marry this man.

CHAPTER 14

"THE ANSWER IS no," blurted Arachne. "I will not marry you."

Leon blinked at her in stunned silence before chortling loudly. Arachne's cheeks blazed, and she had to clench her fists to keep from striking him.

"That's not what I'm proposing," he said, still laughing. "But come to think of it, that might not be a bad idea."

Arachne dropped her arms to her sides and narrowed her eyes at him. Truth be told, she was mortified, but her embarrassment was quickly fading. His nonchalance seemed staged and his laugh nervous. He was up to something. "Absolutely not."

Leon's mask of good humor fell, with his eyebrow dropping almost as quickly as his grin. It took all she had not to smile at him smugly. So, he *had* considered marriage as part of this plan of his, whatever it was, thinking she would be too ignorant or too desperate for a way out of her circumstance to see through his coy ruse.

What a snake. Trying to trick her into being the one to suggest it.

"Well? Out with it!" she snapped, impatient with his games and eager to be on her way. It was getting late. "These rugs aren't going to sell themselves now, are they?"

Leon lifted a finger at her. "Ah, but they could."

Arachne folded her arms again, intrigued. "Is that so?"

Leon looked around, assessing how many ears, if any, were listening. When he was satisfied the alleyways were empty, he leaned in and whispered. "I buy your wares from you and then resell them in my shop."

Arachne gasped, out of indignance or gratitude, she could not say. The last thing she wanted to do was admit Leon's plan might indeed benefit them both, but now that she'd heard it, she couldn't deny it might be exactly what could save her family from their humiliating descent into utter poverty and abject misery.

Leon glanced back at her father's shop, raising both brows after returning his gaze to her. "Athena's tapestry is a display of her power. It is also a warning. No one goes into your shop out of fear of retribution from the gods," began Leon, telling her everything she already knew. "No one will buy from you or your family ever again, Arachne." He clicked his tongue. "When is the last time your mother was commissioned, hmm?"

Arachne stared at him, inhaling deeply before releasing a long and heavy sigh. Leon was more cunning than she had given him credit for. He had backed her into a corner quite easily.

"This is what I propose," said Leon. "Either work with me privately or be forced to sell to me in six full moons publicly. I'm sure the gossip won't be that bad. The choice is yours."

Arachne looked down at her ruined hands. He spoke the truth, and she knew it. As long as Athena's tapestry stood in their shop, broadcasting her victory and serving as a warning of her power, no one would do business with them.

"I'll think about it," she said, picking up the cart.

Leon placed a hand on her shoulder, holding her in place with a squeeze. "Good," he said, his grin returning. "Who knows, perhaps a marriage proposal *will* be on the table one day soon."

Arachne was too stunned to pull away. Instead, she stood frozen as he ran his hand down the length of her arm and around to her elbow before sliding his fingers over her palm and lifting her hand.

"Such a shame," he said, inspecting each crooked finger, turning them this way and that, as though he were selecting vegetables at the market. "The things that one's pride will ruin."

Anger replaced her shock, and she wrenched her hand from his grasp.

He smiled, tilting his head at her. "Don't keep me waiting for your answer too long, Arachne. I'm not sure you or your father can afford it." With that, he turned and headed back to his shop.

Arachne's eyes stung, and her throat thickened, but she gulped down her unshed emotion, refusing to show that Leon's taunts had affected her in any way.

She had always been willful, and it was a hard habit to break. Except, would her stubbornness help or hinder at this point? Was Leon's proposition ridiculous, or was it an answer to her prayers? An arrangement like this would keep them from sinking further into the pit of despair that awaited them. If she agreed, not to the marriage, but to supplying

Leon's shop, who would even know? Her parents would think she went to the market each morning, and when she came back with an empty cart, she would tell them their luck was changing, that she needed more rugs, and bolts of cloth as well. And the townsfolk—did she even care what they thought? They had abandoned her and her family, leaving them to do what they must to survive.

Stomach in knots, she picked up her cart, which suddenly seemed much heavier, and hurried down the street. She usually sat in the hot sun for hours, with no one so much as looking her way let alone buying anything. If she sold one rug today—just one—she would take it as a sign to accept Leon's offer.

Arachne sighed with relief as she tossed the rugs back into the cart. For once, she was happy and smiling that no one had purchased a single thing.

She was resourceful. She would find a different way to make ends meet. In fact, she would sit at the loom that very night and force her hands into submission, no matter how painful. If she pushed herself hard enough, she was sure she could weave once again. Perhaps not as perfect as before, but her worst would be better than most people's best. As for Athena's tapestry, she would simply move it. The goddess had demanded it stay *in* the shop. She had said nothing of *where* it was to be kept. It could be covered and shoved into a dim corner or hidden in a dark storeroom and still be in the shop.

"Wait, miss!"

Arachne looked up to see the girl from that morning rushing towards her.

"I would like to buy one of your rugs," said the girl, breathless from running. "I know my mother would not agree, but the old woman over there said we should be kind to those who have made mistakes, and also help those who have found themselves poor because of their pride." The girl held a small purse out for Arachne to take. "She even gave me the coins."

Arachne's heart hammered in her chest, her gaze frantically darting around the market until she found the old woman the girl spoke of. She was standing off in the distance, holding what looked to be a long stick. One look at the woman's pursed lips and Arachne was sure it was a spear glamoured to appear as a walking staff.

Would Athena ever stop torturing her?

Arachne returned her gaze to the girl and smiled. "Keep the coin." She pulled a rug from her cart and placed it onto the girl's outstretched arms. "I am no beggar."

CHAPTER 15

ARACHNE THREW THE wooden comb down with a grunt. Why would her fingers do as she wished only sometimes, and not all the time? Her mother quickly abandoned her task of folding fabric and rushed over to the loom where Arachne sat weaving—or rather, tried to.

"There's no need to push so hard," said her mother, bending to pick up the weaving tool. "We are selling again. The gods have found it in their hearts to forgive us."

The gods had nothing to do with it. They hadn't forgiven anyone, and they certainly weren't responsible for the family's recent change of circumstance.

What her mother truly meant was the gods had found it in their hearts to forgive her, *Arachne*, not them. But she did not call this to attention, she didn't have the heart to. Instead, she shot up from her stool and placed a hand on her mother's arm and pulled her back up.

"No, no, I'll get it. I was acting like a child."

She shouldn't be exerting herself, thought Arachne as she picked up the comb and inspected it for damage. Her mother should be living out the rest of her days without a care in the world, growing plump on sweet figs, spiced bread with honey, and watered wine, not supporting her grown daughter. Arachne already felt guilty enough for all the pain and suffering she had caused over the past year. She needed to try harder to curb her outbursts.

She sat back down with a huff, trying not to think about her petulance and failing. She was guilty of much more than that. The wool had not run out, but the money for dye had, forcing Arachne to reconsider Leon's offer. Not of marriage, of course, but to supply him with rugs, bolts of fabric, and if her hands would comply soon, tapestries.

For a month now, she had been loading her cart the evening before, so that she could leave before dawn a few mornings each week. She would slip out while her parents slept, letting them believe that she had gone to the market. Of course, that wasn't where she was going. She was meeting with Leon in secret, in an alley. Although the ruse filled her with worry, and even a little shame, she told herself she wasn't being wholly untruthful. Someone *was* buying their wares. She just hadn't disclosed *who*.

But that didn't matter. She had gotten them into this mess, and now she would get them out. She would do whatever it took for her and her parents to thrive once more. She just wished it didn't involve keeping things from them. But it did, and her only consolation was this: The omission of information was a means to an end.

A good one, she hoped, for she had a plan of her own. She would rebuild her reputation, even if it took years. She would move in silence, laying the foundation of her comeback thread by thread. She would labor until her fingers obeyed her commands once again, and she could weave tapestries as beautiful and breathtaking as she had before. And then, when the time was right, she would reveal the tapestries Leon sold in his shop had been woven by Arachne, the best weaver in all of Lydia.

Luckily, Leon had proven to be a discreet businessman so far, and he always paid as promised. As far as she knew, she wasn't getting swindled, and for that, she was thankful.

She sent her mother a smile, hoping it reassured her there was nothing more amiss than a small bout of frustration due to the malfunction of her hands. To her relief, it did, and her mother went back to folding, humming as she arranged the bolts and draped the cloth.

Small as it was, Arachne's smile was another lie, but she pushed it from her mind and continued her weaving. She would not dwell on how her reputation had once preceded her, or how easily fame and fortune had come to her.

That was before getting ensnared by a goddess.

Arachne had been a fool; she could see that now. How different might it all have turned out if she had swallowed her pride and acquiesced, let Athena win, stroked her ego so that she would leave Hypeapa flattered. Had Arachne had the good sense to have done that, she might still be famous instead of infamous.

CHAPTER 16

PIGEONS COOED FROM their perches, joining in the chorus of clacking hooves and creaking wheels as Arachne pulled her empty cart over the cobblestone. She was heading home now, but earlier that morning she had waited in the alleyway nearest Leon's shop before the sun had risen. After he had given the signal—a soft whistle followed by two clicks—that it was indeed him approaching, they had worked in silence to transfer the goods from her cart into large grain sacks, which he had then packed onto the back of a mule.

It was obvious he thought the pre-dawn darkness hid the dubious look in his eyes every time he dropped the silver coins into her palm, but Arachne always saw it as clear as day. This morning, there had been something else, not in his eyes but on his lips; a lopsided grin bordering on a smirk.

She had dismissed it, like always, taking it for smugness at having the upper hand in their arrangement. She had also ignored the niggling feeling that he was up to something, pushing it to the back of her mind and hurrying off to help her sister-in-law for the afternoon. She would tend to her ailing grandfather until the sun was low enough in the sky to return home without suspicion, and then she would weave for the rest of the evening.

Her first tapestry since the contest with Athena would be finished soon, and when it was, she would sell it to Leon. He already profited handsomely from the fabric and rugs, but Arachne knew he would jump at the chance to offer tapestries to his wealthy patrons once more. They had been having to wait longer and travel farther since Athena had condemned Arachne and would surely pay extra for the convenience of not having to send a servant far and away.

Travel was expensive.

She left the cart outside in the work yard, waving to her father as she passed by him on her way inside the shop. The stench of rotting shellfish permeated the air, even though the days were growing cooler and less humid. Her father's vigorous dredging of the fetid water certainly didn't help. In fact, it brought on a wave of nausea, and along with it, some thoughts that were equally unpleasant.

Was she negotiating with Leon for her parents' sakes? Or was she doing it for her own, so that she could deliver some sort of twisted revenge? She assumed once the town discovered he was getting the textiles they paid good money for from a family being punished by the gods, his shop would stand empty like theirs. And if that happened, they would all be in a worst predicament than they were now.

Would she bite the hand that fed her? Was this what being humiliated had done to her? Had she turned into a vengeful and conniving woman seeking retribution, even if it meant losing what little they had? Had her mind truly gotten so warped, her integrity so corrupt?

"Daughter," said her father, scattering her thoughts. He laid down the long wooden stick he used to push the cloth down at the edge of the dyeing pit before making his way over to her.

"I have good news," he said. "Our fortune has changed."

Arachne's stomach dropped when she saw how tentative his smile was, as though he were trying to make himself believe his own words.

"How so?" she replied.

"Leon, the shopkeeper from down the way, has asked for your hand."

Her mind raced; every smile Leon had sent her as he'd pulled out his coins flashed behind her eyes. Once again, she'd been too focused on the future she hadn't seen what was right in front of her. Every enticing coin, every crooked smile, Leon had been biding his time, waiting until her guard was down to pull the net closed.

She swayed on her feet, but her father caught her before she lost her balance.

"It is a good match," he said, holding her steady. "For you and for us."

"Us?" she murmured, not wanting to know the answer but asking anyway.

"Yes, Arachne, for all of us," he answered. "Not only will he take you into his home, but he also promised me and your mother many grandchildren, so that we may have apprentices to carry on our work."

Apprentices? Is that how Leon had positioned it? More like cash cows in training. Any descendants would be nothing more than employees.

Arachne shrugged out of her father's grasp. "You should have come to me first." Panic rose in her throat. "I have already made a deal with him! Where do you think he gets his rugs from? How do you think we have made ends meet this long? If I marry him, we have no more bargaining power."

"Bargaining power? For what?" asked her father, his hands flying into the air. "Do you think I don't know my own daughter? Do you think..." He lowered his voice. "Do you think I don't know where he gets his merchandise?" He gestured toward the shop, where her mother stood in the doorway wrapping her shawl tighter around her shoulders. "We are doomed, Arachne! Nothing will make them buy from us. Not directly, and not so long as they live. We will be dead and gone before the memory of our disgrace fades. This marriage is the only way to salvage our dignity."

"No," replied Arachne, shaking her head. "No, I will repair our damaged reputation and—"

He grabbed hold of her shoulders and shook. "There is no fixing what your foolish pride has destroyed!"

There it was. His true feelings. All this time, resentment had been festering underneath the love and patience and forgiveness. He blamed her and her alone for their misfortune. If she had not challenged Athena, none of this—the lies, the torment, the loss of their livelihood—would have come to pass.

It was true, every bit of it, and the tears Arachne had been fighting fell when her father released her and took a step backward.

"It is done," he said, his voice weak, the look in his eyes begging her not to argue any further. "You are to be married during *gamelion,* and the shop is to be your dowry."

Arachne said nothing as she watched her father walk back to the putrid smelling dye pit to continue his work. Leon had betrayed her, going behind her back to cut himself an even more favorable deal, knowing that every silver coin he gave to her would eventually go right back into his coffers. This wasn't a marriage for love, it was a business venture.

Worse than that, her father hadn't been duped. He hadn't fallen for the trap she'd so carefully avoided, but agreed to it knowing full well it wasn't something Arachne would ever want. And now she would be forced to bear baby after baby while her aging parents were beholden to work their fingers to the bone, all to make a despicable man—her husband, if he got his way—even richer.

CHAPTER 17

ARACHNE RUBBED HER aching head. Empty belly roiling too fiercely to fill, she'd excused herself from the evening meal and retired to the room she used to share with her siblings. It seemed much bigger now that they were gone, lonelier too. What she wouldn't give to curl up next to her sister once more, like when they were children, drifting off to the soothing sounds of night.

But not even the rhythmic chirping of crickets could lull her to sleep now, and so her mind raced. How could she stop this madness? Was there a way to control her own fate?

After tossing and turning for hours, Arachne decided there was only one thing left to do. She would go to Leon with a proposal of her own, acting as her own *kyrios* and re-negotiating the terms of her marriage and dowry herself.

Or at least, she would try.

She felt under her mattress for the scroll she had removed from the chest where her father kept his important documents earlier that afternoon. While her parents were both occupied, she had gone looking for the deed to the shop. What she had planned to do with it, she still didn't know. Perhaps she'd simply wanted to confirm it remained in his possession, that he had not already given it to Leon as some act of good faith while he convinced her the marriage was a good match. When she'd noticed a larger scroll, tucked alongside the deed, she had opened it. According to the date, she'd discovered her father had drawn up the terms of her betrothal some time ago.

She had pressed her lips tight as she'd read over the contract, one part in particular making her jaw clench: *The issue of at least one male child. If there is no male heir produced, the groom may take a concubine to ensure his bloodline is continued.*

Arachne had gritted her teeth. A woman may not be privy to the terms of her marriage, but the one condition she *could* count on was pregnancy. And why not a daughter? *If* Leon and Arachne were to have a child together and it was born a girl, their daughter would undoubtedly have a talent for weaving. The part about the concubine had to have been upon Leon's insistence, to allow his wandering eye to roam, excusing all his future infidelities.

She had pushed away the horrid thought before it could consume her, for any wife or daughter of Leon's would not be cherished but treated as property. This contract proved as much.

Arachne quickly scanned the rest of the terms until she found what she was looking for; the fate of her father's shop: *Upon the marriage of Arachne of Hypeapa and Leon of Colophon, all property and assets of the bride's father, Idmon of Lydia, will be granted to the groom.*

"No," she'd whispered out loud, shaking her head as if it would have made the truth any less unbearable. It was at that point she had stopped herself from marching over to the hearth and ripping the contract to shreds before tossing it onto the banked, but still very hot, coals to burn. Instead, she had gently curled it up, retied the thin leather strip, and stuffed it into a pocket sewn into the folds of her peplos.

Now, her fingers searched beneath the mattress to make sure it was still where she'd hidden it. When they brushed against the thick paper, she pulled them away, as though it had snapped fearsome jaws at her.

She rolled onto her back with a huff. How long ago had Leon asked for her hand? Had her father seen the writing on the wall from the beginning and thought he'd had no choice but to agree to a betrothal? Both of their signatures were already at the bottom. Why had her father waited so long to tell her? It seemed he was keeping some secrets of his own.

Like father, like daughter.

Tears spilled from the corners of her eyes, sliding down her face to soak the hair trapped under her neck. She laid there, wide awake and tormented by the knowledge she was the reason they were nearly destitute and now in need of rescue.

After a while, she wiped away the tears, still feeling betrayed but understanding why her father had decided to join forces instead of working against them. His hands were tied, for he would have never been forced to give away the shop as her dowry if she had just let Athena win.

Arachne swiped the last of the wetness from her eyes, resolved to do what she must to solve the problem she'd created. She was the source of all their pain and suffering, and she must end it. First, she would make sure the shop stayed in her father's name, and that not only would they remain the sole supplier, but that he and her mother got a fair split of everything sold. To do that, she would promise Leon anything. She would tell him whatever he wanted to hear, however untrue, including that she would bear him children. All she needed was for him to agree to the new terms of their marriage.

She inhaled a breath as she pulled the contract from under her mattress. In the end, it wouldn't matter what she promised him.

Arachne slipped out from under the covers, shivering as she dressed. It was still harvesting season and was getting colder outside. January—the month for marriage—was nearly upon them. She had no time to wait, she must take matters into her own hands now, for it was not likely lightning would strike Leon dead any time soon.

She lit a brazier and took out her ink. She must carry out her plan with haste, so that her mother and father would not become servants to Leon's greed.

Once the terms were rewritten, she put on her veil and cloak. When the ink was dry, she tied the scroll and tucked it into a satchel before making her way out of her room and into the shop. She collected one other item she would need before stepping out into the cold, dark night. Arms full, she walked to her cart, carefully placing one foot in front of the other so she wouldn't slip and fall on the frost-slickened cobblestones. It would do no good to break her neck now. Not before Leon agreed to the last deal she would ever make with him.

CHAPTER 18

THE AIR WAS crisp, pinking Arachne's cheeks, already stinging from salty tears. With only the full moon to light her way, Arachne trudged along with her cart.

Leon was already there, slinking into the shadows as she approached. Normally, she was the first to arrive, and she was earlier than usual this morning. Her heart quickened. Had he been waiting there all night?

She blew a soft whistle before clicking her tongue twice.

"Hello, Arachne," murmured Leon, stepping forward. "I wondered if you would come."

"Why wouldn't I?" she began, arching a brow as she pushed past Leon to pull the cart into the alley. "We have an agreement, don't we?" She let go of the cart and spun around to face him. "Or is it my father you prefer to deal with?"

Surprise flashed across his face. After a few beats, he recovered enough to interrogate her with a question of his own. "Well?"

A shiver ran down her spine, and she folded her arms to disguise it. "Well, what?"

He took a step backward, the silvery glow of the moon tinged with the golden light of dawn illuminating his arched brows. "Did I make a good deal?"

He was eager for her answer, but Arachne couldn't care less. There was no chance of happiness with this man. Not after betraying her like this. Had he ever respected her, or had he simply found pleasure in letting her believe so? Arachne decided it was the latter, and now he was only curious to know whether she would make the marriage an easy or a difficult one.

"It seems I have no choice in the matter," she said, an edge of bitterness sharpening her tone.

"No." He dropped his hands to his sides, momentarily disappointed at her reaction before drawing himself up again and squaring his shoulders. "No, I'm afraid you don't."

He sounded stern but looked pathetic. A weak man, posturing so she would not give him trouble. She wasn't so naïve to think the man possessed a single ounce of strength or loyalty. No, she would not fall for his trickery. He was a polecat, wily and sneaky, and certainly incapable of caring about anything other than the wealth he would amass.

He opened his mouth to speak, but she cut him off before he could say another word. "I come to renegotiate the contract," she said, reaching inside her satchel to pull out the scroll.

One of Leon's eyebrows slid up. "This is not Sparta." He huffed an incredulous laugh that made Arachne's blood boil. "Women don't have a say in Lydia."

Leon was laughing heartily now, but Arachne tamped her anger down, resisting the urge to strike him. Instead, she reached for the cloth that covered the back of her cart.

Sweeten your tone, she told herself. *You will catch more bees with honey than vinegar.*

"They do if they can weave like this," she said softly, lifting the edge of the cloth and revealing the key to her bargaining power.

It wasn't perfect, but it was finer than any tapestry that could be bought in the nearby towns or villages. If Leon agreed to refuse her father's shop as a dowry because he thought there would be more to come, she would let him.

Leon suddenly stopped laughing. Arachne held her breath when he stepped toward the cart and threw off the rest of the cloth. He pulled the tapestry out for a closer look, running his hand over it and leaning closer still.

"I need more light to inspect the craftsmanship," he insisted before quickly rolling up the tapestry and hoisting it over his shoulder.

Arachne was annoyed, but she did not protest, only walked behind him silently as he hurried down the road, holding in his arms the true reason he was so eager to take her as his wife.

Leon had already lit a lamp and was holding it over her work when Arachne entered his shop. His brow furrowed as his eyes darted across the intricate design. He was looking for imperfections, and it twisted her stomach in knots, but once she saw his eyes go wide, and his smile flash even wider because he'd found none, her worries vanished.

After that, all it took was the arch of her brow and the promise of more tapestries for Arachne to leave with a binding contract. Her father would remain Leon's sole supplier, and no matter what happened to Arachne, whether she lived a long life, or the furies dragged her to the Underworld tomorrow, the shop would stay in his name. Not only that, but the farm that had been passed on to her brother would also remain in the family.

A satisfied smile curled Arachne's lips as she pushed her empty cart home. It had been easier to act as her own *kyrios* than she had thought. Leon had been so focused on his own gain, and the future profits he thought he would make off her, he hadn't needed much convincing. Although she'd had a moment of doubt when Leon had belittled her, it had only hardened her resolve. And she was proud of that.

But her smile quickly faded, her heart growing heavy, for there was still one thing she must do. Something that would finally set all the wrong she'd done right.

CHAPTER 19

The Next Morning

THE SUN WAS just beginning to rise when Arachne approached the farm. *It is done*, she thought as she unlatched the gate, *they are all safe from ruin and now I can...*

She waved at her brother, already up and letting the sheep out of their enclosure. He greeted her before whistling sharply at a pair of dogs. The hounds jumped to their feet, taking off after the sheep without hesitation, nipping at their wooly flanks as they herded them further into the pasture.

Go in peace.

Arachne placed a hand on her satchel protectively and continued toward the house. She tried ignoring the sound of a hundred bleating sheep as they were driven farther away from the safety of their pen, but the task was difficult. They were not in control of their lives, and she could relate.

If only she had remained part of the flock and ignored her yearning to break away. If she had come into this world unremarkable, with ordinary skills, and even more mundane aspirations, perhaps she wouldn't have dared to stand out. She certainly wouldn't have had the audacity to challenge a goddess.

But what of her driving need for justice, or her infallible sense of right and wrong? What about the things that were innate, and not learned? Even if she had possessed no talent for weaving, she very well may have found herself as cast down as she was now, for she couldn't stop being who she was, not only in her heart but her soul.

It would have been better if I had never been born at all.

Arachne bit the inside of her lip to distract herself from the unrelenting thoughts regaling her mind, but they still came. First, how she had taken the shredded pieces of her tapestry from the basket the previous evening and tied them together until they'd formed a long strip. For days there had been a voice inside her mind, reminding her how full of sorrow she would always be, living in a world where she had failed herself and others so miserably.

It whispered to her, telling her of the terrible numbness consuming her, and how it would not stop until who she was before was gone. It had told her how the sadness that had settled in her bones would never go away. It spoke of honor and atonement while she coiled the rope and stowed it in her satchel with the herbs for the tea that soothed her grandfather's pain.

"I'm going to help with grandfather," she had said, kissing her mother on the cheek and wrapping her arms around her shoulders before leaving that morning.

Her mother had leaned into the embrace. "All will be well," she'd said, reaching up to pat Arachne's cheek.

Arachne had squeezed her mother tight, memorizing the feel of her. "Yes, all will be well."

When she'd broken away, her mother had said, "It vexes me to see you and your father at odds."

Arachne had nodded as she'd swallowed around the lump in her throat. "I know I left him with no choice. I will talk to him before I go."

And she had, forgiving him for doing what he thought would stop his family's name falling further from grace by arranging a marriage of convenience to save the name she had tarnished. When she had embraced him, she'd said a silent prayer that he would be able to forgive her as she had him.

She inhaled deeply, once again pushing away her thoughts as she entered the small home of her brother and his wife, Elena.

"Oh, thank the gods you're here," said Elena, nursing her newborn son. She ticked her head toward the back room where Arachne's grandfather lay bedridden. "He's more ornery than usual this morning."

Arachne found the will to laugh, though barely. She felt sorry for Elena. After this day, she would have to take care of the new and helpless as well as the old and helpless on her own.

She put water over the fire and waited for it to boil so she could make her grandfather's mountain tea. "You and Neleos are well matched, Elena." Arachne spooned the herbs into a sachet and tied it tight. "It makes my heart happy."

"Mine, as well," said Elena, gently brushing a thumb over her baby's cheek. "Your brother is a good man."

Arachne poured steaming water into a cup before setting the kettle on the hearth stone, wishing she would have been born as humble as her brother. It had done him well, for he had been rewarded with all the things that truly mattered in this world. "Nisos will have a good life."

"And so will your children, Arachne," replied Elena. Her sentiment was lighthearted and hopeful, but Arachne still felt the doubt, and perhaps even pity, belying her sister-in-law's words.

Arachne smiled as she nodded, refusing to betray her true feelings. She would never bring children into this world because she would never marry.

"You are the bravest woman I know," said Elena, rocking a milk drunk Nisos to sleep.

Arachne's chest tightened, and her throat ached from holding back tears. It wasn't true, but it was kind of Elena to say, and it made Arachne almost change her mind.

"You're too kind, Elena. I do what I must for the family. I am a too big a fool to do anything else." Arachne stared at the steam rising from the cup. "Enough of this sentimental talk. You know I don't do well with it. I'm going to give grandfather his tea, and then I must go feed the hens."

"You are a good woman, Arachne," said Elena.

Arachne resisted the urge to scream. She wasn't good, not anymore. Maybe not ever.

She picked up the tea, smiling at Elena as she left the room to hide the fact that in just six words, Elena had pushed Arachne over the edge.

CHAPTER 20

ARACHNE STOOD AT the edge of the loft, heart hammering painfully in her chest as she peered down. Everything looked so small from this high up. She shivered, gooseflesh raising on her arms. Was this how Athena saw the world when she came down from her place of power and privilege in the sky?

The hay was soft beneath her feet, but Arachne doubted the dirt below would be as forgiving. Her head throbbed, and her stomach twisted, but she took comfort in knowing that soon she would feel nothing.

That it would only hurt for a moment, and then there would be no more pain.

Her mother's words echoed in her mind as she slid a hand into her satchel. *All will be well.* Yes, her mother and father would be well... eventually.

She pulled out the braided remains of her finest tapestry. A wave of sorrow nearly sent her scrambling back down to safer ground, but she resisted the urge to run away from her atonement. She would rather cease to exist than let a wretched man like Leon take what little they had left. Not when there was another way out, and not just for her, but for them all.

She only wished she would have realized sooner, before she had gone to Leon; if there was no woman to marry, there would be no dowry to lose.

After returning home, something still hadn't felt right, but it had eluded her, only coming to her in a dream. In her dream, she sat at her loom, every thread she tried to weave falling through her hands like sand until there was a pile at her feet. She'd gasped when the threads knitted themselves together and cried out when they'd coiled around her body like vines. She woke with a start when they had squeezed her so tight she couldn't breathe. Her hand had gone to her throat, and as she had gulped down air, the meaning had become clear. Athena's punishment would never stop. She would never be allowed to forget her mistake, forever seeking forgiveness for her sins.

She carefully tied one end of the rope to the beam above her head. She had to stand on her toes to reach it, but she managed. When she was done, and the other end was around her neck, she closed her eyes, steeling herself with a deep breath before clenching her teeth. She balled her hands into fists and flexed the muscles that would launch her into freedom, for she would rather meet a quick ending than live a long and suffering life.

"Stop," came a loud voice, one she had heard before but did not recognize. "I command you."

Arachne froze, every muscle obeying the order except for one; her heart. Her eyelids popped open at the same time her heart exploded in her chest, causing her to lurch forward. She would have toppled from the loft if she hadn't steadied herself by grabbing onto the rope above her head out of reflex.

Athena stood before Arachne, who teetered on both the edge of the loft and her sanity. The goddess loomed tall enough for Arachne to look in her cold, gray eyes and meet her even colder gaze. She had not come disguised as the old woman, but as her true self, in a pristine white chiton and gleaming gold armor.

"Why?" began Arachne, not knowing what else to say. "Isn't this what you wanted? To humiliate me so deeply, to put me in my place so thoroughly that I would seek to end the suffering myself?"

"Hubris has consequences," replied Athena. "The day you challenged me is the day you sealed your fate, Arachne. Your life is no longer yours to do with as you please. It is not yours to take because it belongs to me.”

“What is left? You have taken it all!” cried Arachne. “Because of a mistake I made, one you didn’t allow me to make right!”

“Examples must be made.” Athena lifted her chin. “Pride must be punished.”

No longer able to hold them back, Arachne released her tears. They flooded down her face, taking with them what little will to live she had left. “What of forgiveness?” She dropped her hands from the rope, letting them hang limply at her sides. “Was there no grace to be given? Are the gods so blinded in their vision they cannot see regret? Are they so elevated by their wisdom they forget that humans are not perfect? So hardened to the plight of man they forget to be generous in their mercy?” Arachne inched closer to the edge of the beam. “You speak to me of consequences, yet you suffer none. You abuse your power because of jealousy and wounded pride, and then lecture me on hubris? Oh, the hypocrisy! The only difference between you and I, goddess? You were born a daughter of Zeus, and I was not.”

Arachne hadn’t expected to get through to her, but Athena’s throat bobbed. Could it be her pride the goddess had just swallowed? Even if it was, it didn't matter now. Arachne's faith was gone, her spirit crushed into too many pieces for her to ever be the same.

There was no going back, only forward.

"You are no better than a powerless human—none of you are," she continued, moving so the balls of her feet rested on the edge and her toes hung over it. "You keep your secrets hidden with fear of punishment, but I know what you do not want revealed. I've seen your true nature, for you've shown me with clarity just how pathetic and insecure you are and always will be. You can tarnish my name, you can deny me grace, you can even claim to be a better weaver... but you will *never* strip me of my dignity."

Arachne stepped off the ledge. As the ground rose up to meet her, Athena's deafening scream went quiet. And with a flash of blinding light, the world as Arachne knew it was no more.

CHAPTER 21

Arachne braced for impact, and even though a shattering pain seized her body, it never came. Instead, she was pulled up short before spinning in dizzy circles as she hung limply above the hard-packed earth. When she realized she was dangling upside down, she reached for the rope to pull herself upright, so that she could set her feet on the ground. Her stomach dropped when she discovered it was not a rope at all, but a thin and sticky thread of silk.

Despite her disorientation, she found the strength to climb the thread, where she clung trying to puzzle out why the world seemed so different; everything looked enormous, as if she had shrunk. Panic bubbled in her belly when Athena looked down at her, clearing her confusion with the barest hint of a smug smile on her lips.

"A spider," said the goddess. "Not a dog, nor bird, nor snake. A spider, small and dreadful to all those who encounter you."

No, no, no, no, no!

Of course, Athena would not admit defeat, nor would she let her grudge against Arachne go, instead cursing her to live as something frightening, that creeped and crawled underfoot. But no tears came to Arachne's eyes at this revelation, for spiders did not cry. Nor did they sleep. They wove their webs, they watched, and then they withered.

But Arachne was cursed. She would never die.

Arachne tried to scream, but no sound came out. And as Athena vanished into thin air with a satisfied snicker, she scurried into a corner, clinging to the rough wood with her eight long and gangly appendages.

She stayed there for hours, cowering in the dark. Only when she had been sure the goddess would not come back to squash her between a palm or beneath a foot, she had taken stock of her new body. It was tiny, and her arms were many and covered in hideous hair. Or were they legs? Whatever they were, they were no longer human.

She no longer had hands, with fingers to grip, but at least they no longer caused her pain when she manipulated the silk threads that came out of her midsection. It was the one good thing that had come of it; she could weave again, but even faster and more beautifully than when she was mortal. And weave she did. She covered the barn in her webs, and although there were plenty of wondrous works to behold, no one came to see her handiwork.

She did not know how long it had been, but she began to miss her parents, and even though it would take her many weeks to make the perilous journey back to the shop, she climbed down from the rafters. When she saw her brother sheering the sheep, she scurried into the wood pile to wait for him to fill the freshly shorn wool into the empty linen sacks hung on iron hooks.

She would travel safely tucked inside the wool. If she could have, she would have laughed at her brilliant plan to avoid hiding in dark places during the day, dodging trampling hooves and stomping feet to get to the underside of a leaf or into the crannies of a woodpile. And then there were the birds and wasps that hunted during the day, poking their sharp beaks and pinching jaws into the cracks if she so much as moved. Nor would she have at to be wary of scorpions searching for their prey when the sun went down.

After many days, she finally arrived at her parents' home. She crawled up the wall to the rafters, where she weaved her webs. She spun one in every corner. She weaved so many her mother would often curse as she swept them away with a broom.

How fitting, thought Arachne every time she rebuilt her web, *that I should be allowed to weave so skillfully and so beautifully, just to be forced to relive the destruction of my work for all eternity.*

THE END

The Author

Forever a fan of fairytales, folklore, and mythology, Kerri brings life to the mythological characters you know and love... or love to hate.

Kerri lives in Michigan with her husband, son and cat they lovingly but aptly refer to as The Maleficence. Mel for short. If Kerri isn't raking leaves or shoveling snow, she's either reading, writing or has fled her evil to-do list and fallen down an Internet rabbit hole... Or possibly just fallen and can't get up.

For news and updates about upcoming releases, sign up for Kerri's newsletter at kerrikeberly.com. For an inside look at the day in the life of a crafty crochet-addicted, DIY-loving, Greek mythology-obsessed author, follow her on Facebook, Instagram, and TikTok.

www.ingramcontent.com/pod-product-compliance
Lightning Source LLC
Chambersburg PA
CBHW030903200726
48289CB00003B/878